Dining & Entertaining Maggie O' Style

Pamela Boleyn

Pamela Boleyn

ISBN: 978-1-961485-94-5 Paperback

FV-9
To contact the author:
Boleyn Books
P. O. Box 2592
Daphne, Alabama 36526

www.BoleynBooks.com

DEDICATION

*To My Mother, Maxine,
Who taught me how to cook and entertain.*

Pamela Boleyn

CONTENTS

"Good food is very often, even most often, simple food."

Anthony Bourdain

For Starters

When reading my book *Maggie O'-Seven Years Forgotten*, you will find several steamy scenes that are not only about sex, but also about the bond that can take place when you share a meal with someone special. Many first dates take place at a bar or restaurant. Sharing food and drinks helps break the ice. And if the intimacy has a chance to grow, you will continue to go out for dinner dates and to celebrate special occasions.

But perhaps even better than enjoying a table for two at a romantic restaurant, is to wake up in the morning and your lover prepares a divinely delicious breakfast for you. Recall how Maggie's lovers-Ron, Sean, and John-were as good in the kitchen as they were in the bedroom. I personally admit that when I'm initially attracted to someone, and they also enjoy cooking for me, my attraction factor for them multiples.

Thinking back to how many romantic food scenarios described in my first Maggie O' novel, has inspired me to write this dining and entertaining guide. Also, I should mention, in addition to loving writing, I love to cook, and I operate a small catering business with my boyfriend, who is an amazing chef. He has encouraged me to pursue my dreams as both a writer and chef.

I hope my Maggie O' Style guide will help you plan and enjoy special romantic dinners or any other dining focused event

The #1 Maggie O' Entertaining Tip:
Never overload yourself when you entertain.

Your guests will most likely sense your discomfort. The only thing worse than going to a bad dinner party, is throwing one.

- It's better to have a small party of positive people than a larger party which includes a few downers.

- Do not complicate the menu. You don't have to make everything from scratch.

- Prep as much ahead. Invite a friend to help.

- Do not freak out if everything is not perfect.

- Keep the adult beverage glasses full.

- Use candles and fresh flowers to set the mood.

- Play background music to match your party theme.

- K.I.S.S. – Keep it simple, sweetie.

Helpful Cooking Tips

- Read the recipe all the way through before you start. Make sure you have all the required ingredients and enough time to prepare it.

- Measure and chop your ingredients before you start cooking. Known as *mise en place*, French for "everything in its place."

- Put a damp paper or kitchen towel under your cutting board. This prevents it from moving around while you are cutting.

- Make sure your cutting knives are properly sharpened. It makes slicing and chopping easier, whereas a dull knife can slip and accidentally cut you.

- Not all ovens cook the same. To prevent overcooking, set your timer for a few minutes earlier than the time indicated in the recipe. You can always cook longer if needed.

- Invest in a good digital instant-read meat thermometer to ensure the meat is cooked to the proper temperature and is safe to eat. Also, you do not want to ruin meat by overcooking it.

- Mince garlic by hand, it's much cheaper and more flavorful than the jar kind.

- Let meat rest after cooking and before cutting. This allows the juices to reabsorb into the meat. Rest thin cuts 5-7 minutes and thicker cuts 15-20 minutes.

- Season and taste as you go. Don't wait to taste until the end.

- If you don't have a cooking thermometer to check the oil temperature, drop a small piece of bread into the oil. If the bread sinks to the bottom of the pan, the oil is too cold. If it burns immediately, it's too hot. If it sizzles slowly, it's just right.

- It's important to have your cream at room temperature before you mix it into a hot sauce, so it does not curdle.

- Some recipes call for a dash of an ingredient. A dash is a measure of less than 1/8 teaspoon.

- When a recipe ingredient has "divided" next to it, it means that the ingredient will be added to the recipe in parts and not in the entire measurement listed.

Dining & Entertaining Maggie O' Style

*"A recipe has no soul.
You as the cook must bring soul to the recipe."*

Thomas Keller

1

Magnolia Springs Dinner at Ron's

Kahlúa Pecan Brie

Buttermilk Fried Oyster Caesar Salad

Shrimp and Grits

Strawberry Margarita Key Lime Pie

Maggie and Sean were invited to Ron's Magnolia Springs riverfront cottage. As in the early days of the Magnolia Springs settlement, mail and most packages are still delivered by boat to the houses' docks.

Ron enjoys using locally sourced seafood and produce when he cooks. He had shopped the day before, picking up fresh oysters and shrimp from his favorite local seafood purveyor, along with pecans, strawberries, and Romaine lettuce from a local farmer's market.

The Key Lime Pie and the Caesar Dressing can be prepared the day before.

Easy to serve, Ron's Shrimp and Grits casserole is a perfect choice when entertaining. Prep the day before, then assembly and bake, just before dinner time.

Kahlúa Pecan Brie

¾ cup finely chopped pecans
¾ cup packed brown sugar
¼ cup Kahlúa
1 (14 ounce) whole Brie cheese
Apple slices
Assorted crackers

Preheat oven 350 degrees F. Spread the pecans in a 9-inch glass pie plate. Microwave on high for 4 to 6 minutes or until toasted, stirring every 2 minutes. Add brown sugar and Kahlúa and stir to mix well. Remove the rind from the top of the Brie and place cheese in a small baking dish. Spoon the pecan mixture evenly over the Brie. Bake 15 to 20 minutes. Serve with assorted crackers and apple slices.

Recommended wines: *Chardonnay or Riesling*

Ron's Favorite Caesar Dressing

2 garlic cloves minced
1 teaspoon anchovy paste
2 tablespoons of freshly squeezed lemon juice
1 teaspoon of Zatarian's Creole Mustard
1 teaspoon of Worcestershire sauce
1 cup of Duke's Real Mayonnaise
½ cup freshly grated Parmigiano-Reggiano Cheese
¼ teaspoon salt
¼ teaspoon black pepper

In a medium bowl, whisk the garlic, anchovy paste, lemon juice, Dijon mustard and Worcestershire sauce. Add the mayonnaise, cheese, salt and pepper.

Buttermilk Fried Oysters
Serves 6 Entrée portions

Fried oysters are also great on top of a Caesar Salad
48 fresh shucked oysters, drained and patted dry
1 cup whole buttermilk
2 tablespoon Tabasco
1 ½ cups plain yellow cornmeal
¾ cup all-purpose flour
1 tablespoon + 1 teaspoon Creole seasoning
Peanut or vegetable oil

Stir buttermilk and Tabasco in a medium bowl. Add oysters to mixture and let marinate for 15 minutes. Place cornmeal, flour, and creole seasoning in a shallow glass pan or pie plate, and whisk together. Remove oysters one at a time and dredge in cornmeal mixture. After shaking off excess, place on a metal cooking rack. Let rest while oil heats. Place a Dutch oven on medium heat and pour in 2 inches of oil. When oil reaches 350 degrees F (use a deep-fry thermometer to test) add in oysters, approximately 12 oysters at a time, careful not to overcrowd the pan! Fry
for 2 to 3 minutes, when
breading is golden brown
and edges are slightly curled.
Using a slotted spoon
remove from oil and place
on a wire cooling rack to
drain. Repeat in batches,
making sure that oil remains
at 350 degrees F. Best served
with Cocktail Sauce,
Remoulade, or Tartar Sauce.

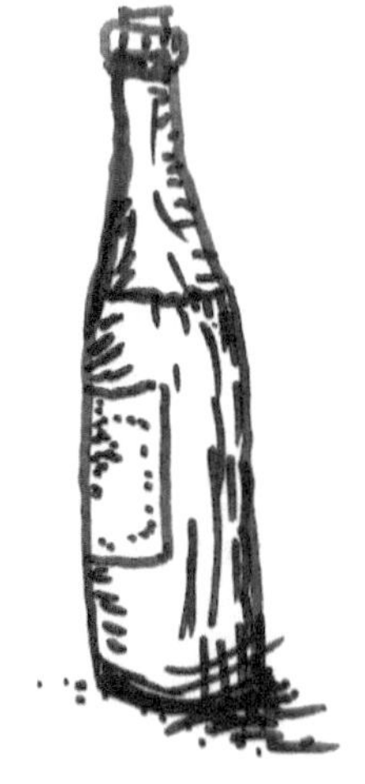

Recommended wines:
*Riesling or Cabernet
Sauvignon*

Shrimp and Grits Casserole
Serves 8

4 cups of chicken broth
½ teaspoon salt
1 cup regular grits
1 cup of shredded sharp cheddar cheese, divided
1 cup of shredded Monterey jack pepper cheese, divided
2 tablespoons of butter
6 green onions, chopped
1 green bell pepper, chopped
2 garlic cloves
2 pounds fresh small shrimp, peeled and cooked
1 10-ounce can Rotel diced tomatoes & green chilies drained
¼ teaspoon salt
¼ teaspoon pepper

Up to a day ahead: Bring chicken broth and ½ teaspoon of salt to boil in a large saucepan. Stir in grits, cover and reduce heat and simmer 20 minutes, until done. Stir in ¾ cup of cheddar cheese and ¾ cup of Monterey jack cheese. Remove from heat. (Hint: Can cool mixture down and refrigerate until the next day. When ready to cook, remove from the refrigerator and bring to room temp.) Melt butter in a large skillet over medium heat. Add green onions, bell pepper, and garlic and sauté until tender. (Hint: this can also be stored until next day).

On day you wish to serve: Mix together the grits mixture, veggies and shrimp. You may want to add approximately ½ cup of half and half or cream to thin it slightly. Pour into lightly greased 2-quart casserole dish. Sprinkle with remaining cheese. Bake in pre heated 350-degree oven till bubbly, 30-40 minutes.

Recommended wine: *Valpolicella Ripasso or Malbec*

Strawberry Margarita Key Lime Pie
Serves 8

5 egg yolks, beaten
1 (14-ounce) can sweetened condensed milk
½ cup key lime juice (Fresh or Nellie's Key Lime Juice)
1 tablespoon grated lime juice
1(9-inch) prepared graham cracker crust

Note: This easy key lime pie recipe is the 1999 American Pie Council's National Pie Championship's 1st place winner in the Quick and Easy Category. I added the optional Strawberry Margarita Sauce. You could not use the sauce and just garnish each piece with a slice of lime and a dollop of whipped cream.

Preheat oven to 375 degrees F. Combine egg yolks, condensed milk, key lime juice, and lime zest in bowl. Pour into graham cracker crust, place pie on a baking sheet. Bake approximately 15 minutes until the filling is set. Cool for 30 minutes on a cake rack. Chill pie at least 3 hours or overnight before serving. Top with whipped cream and drizzle with Strawberry Margarita Sauce.

Strawberry Margarita Sauce

2 cups of hulled strawberries
3 tablespoons lime juice
1 tablespoon agave or honey
1 tablespoon of tequila

Blend ingredients in blender. If desired refrigerate overnight. Delicious served cold over dessert or on savory dishes like grilled fish or chicken.

"All happiness depends on a leisurely breakfast."

John Gunther

2

Matthew's Bloody Mary Brunch

New York, New York Bagel Station

Maggie's Deviled Eggs

Cheese Grits Casserole

Maman's Nutty Chocolate Chunk Cookies

The Perfect Bloody Mary and Mimosa Bar

Maggie and Matthew hosted Sunday brunch for a dozen of their New York friends. Brunch happens early in the day, so it's important to get as much done the day before. Matthew pre-ordered the bagels and cookies and then picked them up late Saturday afternoon. Maggie prepared her deviled eggs and assembled her casserole on Saturday night at Matthew's apartment. They also prepped and refrigerated as many of the bagel toppings that night as well.

On Sunday they set up a self-serve bagel station on Matthew's Mid-Century side board. A large table or countertop would also work. Just make sure there is a toaster to heat the bagels. If serving full size bagels, plan on 1 ½ bagels per person. For mini bagels, plan on 2 ½ bagels per person.

The Perfect Bloody Mary Bar

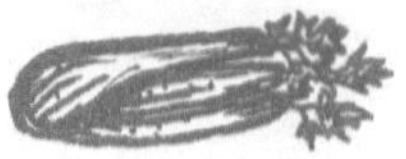

Combine Whiskey Willy's Bloody Mary Mix and Tito's Handmade Vodka to your liking. Then use your imagination and garnish with limes, lemons, celery ribs, blue cheese stuffed olives, bacon strips, boiled shrimp, or anything your heart desires.

New York, New York Bagel Station

Bagels: Everything, Plain, Cinnamon Raisin

Cream Cheese: Plain, Onion, Chive, Honey Walnut

Protein: Smoked Salmon, Crisp Bacon, Black Forest
Ham, Pastrami

Spreads: Whipped Butter, Nutella, Peanut Butter,
Fruit Preserves, Apple Butter

Sliced Veggies: Tomatoes, Red Onions, Cucumber
Greens: Arugula, Spinach

Fruits: Assorted Berries, Sliced Bananas

More treats: Deviled Eggs, Capers, Sliced
Black Olives

Pamela Boleyn

Maggie's Deviled Eggs
12 Halves

6 large eggs
2 tablespoons Dukes Real Mayonnaise
1 ½ tablespoons Wickles Original Relish
1 teaspoon Zatarain's Creole Mustard
1/8 teaspoon salt
Dash of black pepper
Paprika
Pickled Jalapenos for garnish (optional)

Place eggs in a single layer in a saucepan and cover with 1 ½ inches of salted water above the eggs. Heat on high until water boils, then cover, turn heat to low, and cook for 1 minute. Remove from heat and leave covered for 14 minutes. While eggs are cooking, prepare a bowl of ice water. When eggs are done, transfer them to the ice bath. Leave them until they are cool enough to handle, but still warm about 2-3 minutes. Crack each egg all over by tapping it on the counter. Roll the egg gently between your hands to loosen the shell. Under cold running water, peel the egg, starting at the large end. Cut eggs in half and carefully remove the yokes. Mash the yokes with mayonnaise. Add mustard, relish, salt and pepper. Stir well. Spoon egg mixture into halved egg whites. Garnish with paprika. For an added kick, add a pickled jalapeno ring on top.

Cheese Grits Casserole
6-8 Servings

1 cup stone-ground grits
4 cups of water
1 teaspoon of salt
2 cups sharp cheddar, shredded
5 tablespoons unsalted butter
½ cup half and half
2 eggs, lightly beaten

Preheat oven to 350 degrees F. Lightly grease a 2 ½ quart casserole dish. Cook grits according to package directions. When they are done remove from heat and stir in cheese and butter until melted. First stir in the half and half. Stir in a couple of tablespoons of grits into the eggs, to prevent the eggs from curdling. Add egg mix into grits and stir. Add salt and pepper to taste and a dash of garlic powder. Pour into casserole dish and bake 30-40 minutes until set.

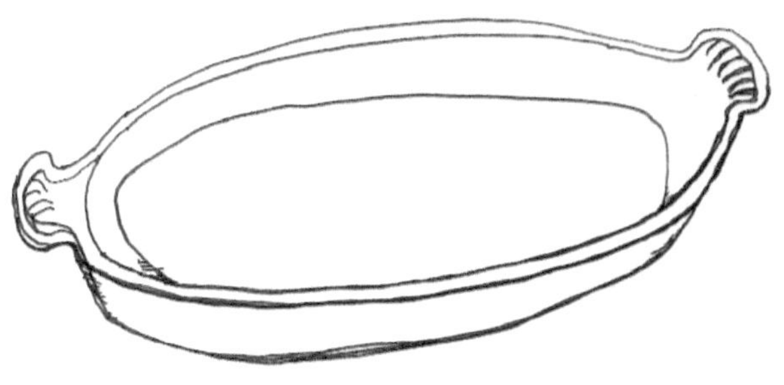

"You don't need a silver fork to eat good food"

Paul Prudhomme

3

Bessie's Kitchen Wisdom & Recipes

Fried Green Tomatoes

Chicken & Conecuh Sausage Gumbo

Creole Mustard Potato Salad

Southern Collard Greens

Buttermilk Cornbread with Honey Butter

*Chilton County Peach Cobbler and Vanilla
Ice Cream*

Maggie once told John, "When I was growing up, I used to watch our housekeeper, Bessie, make gumbo. She made quite a production of it. She would tell me how life and gumbo were so much alike. She said, "Maggie, dear, just like when making a roux you must exercise patience so you don't get burned. And just like in life you should never leave out gumbo's Holy Trinity, bell peppers, onion, and celery."

Bessie also warned Maggie to not overcrowd the iron skillet when frying green tomatoes. If you do, the oil temperature will drop too much and the tomatoes will get soggy. Just like in life, you should never take on more than you can handle.

Bessie's Fried Green Tomatoes

4 medium green tomatoes
1 ½ teaspoons kosher salt divided
1 ½ cups all-purpose flour, divided
½ cup of stone ground cornmeal
½ teaspoon ground black pepper
1/2 cup whole buttermilk
2 large eggs
1 quart vegetable oil
Heaping tablespoon of bacon fat (optional)

Slice tomatoes 1/4 inch thick, discarding the ends. Place sliced tomatoes in a single layer of paper towel and sprinkle with ½ tsp of salt. Place ½ cup of flour in a bowl. In a shallow dish whisk together cornmeal, pepper, 1 cup flour and 1 tsp of salt. In a medium size bowl, whisk buttermilk and eggs together. Dredge tomato slices in flour mix, shaking off excess. Next dredge in buttermilk, letting excess drip off. Last dredge in cornmeal mix. Place on wire rack and let rest for 10 minutes. Heat oil and if desired bacon fat over medium heat in a large cast-iron skillet to 375 degrees F. Fry sliced tomatoes in small batches until crisp and golden brown on one side, then carefully flip and fry on the other side. Transfer to a paper towel-lined pan to drain. Serve with Bessie's Remoulade Sauce.

Bessie's Remoulade Sauce

1 ¼ cup of Duke's Real Mayonnaise
¼ cup Zatarain's Creole Mustard
1 tablespoon sweet paprika
1 teaspoon Cajun seasoning
2 teaspoons prepared horseradish
1 ½ teaspoons sweet pickle juice
1 teaspoon Tabasco
1 clove of garlic minced

Mix ingredients together. Adjust Cajun seasoning to taste. Chill for at least two hours.

This sauce is also great on boiled shrimp, crab cakes, and fried oysters.

Recommended wines: *Sauvignon Blanc or Riesling (medium-dry)*

Pamela Boleyn

Chicken & Conecuh Sausage Gumbo
Serves 10

1 cup of all-purpose flour
1 cup of vegetable oil
1 onion, chopped
2 stalks of celery, chopped
1 green pepper, chopped
4 cloves of garlic minced
4 cups of chicken stock
1 pound of Conecuh sausage, sliced
1 pound of boneless chicken thighs
1 tablespoon of Cajun seasoning
2 bay leaves
Salt and black pepper to taste
2 tablespoons Zatarain's Gumbo File'
6 cups of long-grain white rice
Chopped green onions to garnish

Cut the boneless chicken thighs into small pieces and set aside. In a large Dutch oven, heat the vegetable oil over medium-high heat. Add onions, celery, bell pepper, and garlic. Sauté for 5-7 minutes, or until the vegetables are tender. Add the flour and stir with a wooden spoon constantly on low heat until it turns into a dark brown color, making a roux. Add the chicken stock, Conecuh sausage, boneless chicken thighs pieces, Cajun seasoning, bay leaves, salt, pepper, and file. Bring the gumbo to a boil, then reduce the heat and let it simmer for at least 2-3 hours.   Serve the gumbo hot over bowls of cooked white rice. Garnish with chopped green onions. Serve with Tabasco Sauce.

Recommended wines: *Pinot Noir or Cabernet Sauvignon*

Creole Mustard Potato Salad
Serves 8-10

Best made the day before serving.

1 ½ pounds of russet potatoes peeled and cubed
¼ cup finely chopped celery
3 hard boiled eggs, chopped
½ cup green onion sliced
½ cup of Wickles Pickle Relish
½ cup of Dukes mayonnaise
1 tablespoon Creole Mustard
Salt and pepper to taste
Smoked paprika to garnish

Cook potatoes in a pot with a pinch of salt until done. Approximately 15 minutes. Drain and cool down for about an hour. In a separate bowl make the Creole Mayo Sauce. Mix the mayo, Creole mustard, pickle relish, salt and pepper together. In a large bowl, combine the cooled potatoes, egg, and celery with the Creole Mayo Sauce. Sprinkle paprika to garnish.

Southern Collard Greens
Serves 6

8 ounces smoked bacon
2 pounds of collard greens, washed thoroughly
1 ½ tablespoons minced garlic
1 medium size Vidalia or sweet onion, chopped
48 ounces low-sodium chicken broth
¼ teaspoon of black pepper
¼ teaspoon of white pepper
½ teaspoon kosher salt
1 ½ teaspoons of sugar
3 tablespoons apple cider vinegar

Over medium heat, cook the bacon in a large stockpot until almost crisp. Add onion, and cook until translucent. Stir in garlic and cook 1 minute. Add chicken broth, collard greens, vinegar, sugar, salt, and peppers. Simmer uncovered over low heat about 90 minutes until tender.

Buttermilk Cornbread
Serves 8

2 cups of White Lily cornmeal mix
2 eggs
1 ½ cups whole buttermilk (shake before pouring)
½ stick salted butter melted
2 tablespoons vegetable oil for coating a 9 or 10-inch cast iron skillet

Add oil to a 9 or 10-inch cast iron skillet. Place skillet in oven and begin preheating oven to 450 degrees F. While skillet heats, whisk eggs in large mixing bowl. Whisk in cornmeal, buttermilk, and butter. When oven is preheated, remove pan and pour batter into skillet and return to oven. Bake until top is golden brown and center is done, 15 to 20 minutes. Serve with honey butter.

Hints: For a Mexican Cornbread version, add chopped jalapenos or a can of chopped green chili pepper and a 14.75 ounce can creamed corn and reduce buttermilk to 1 cup.

Pamela Boleyn

Honey Butter

½ cup unsalted butter, room temperature
3 tablespoons honey
½ teaspoon kosher salt

Beat ingredients together until fluffy. Spoon into 4-ounce glass bowl or ramekin. Serve at room temperature. Can be stored in airtight container for up to 2 days.

Chilton County Peach Cobbler
Serves 8-10

2 cups fresh Chilton County peaches, peeled and sliced
½ cup sugar
1 stick of butter
1 cup light brown sugar
½ cup whole milk
1 cup sifted plain flour
1 ½ teaspoons baking powder
¾ teaspoon salt
1 teaspoon nutmeg
2/3 cup finely chopped pecans or walnuts (optional)

Mix peaches with ½ cup sugar and let stand 30 minutes until juices form. Preheat oven 350 degrees F. Put butter in a 2-quart baking dish and place in oven, until butter melts. Make batter of remaining ingredients, except for nuts. Pour batter over butter, then pour peaches including juice over the batter. DO NOT STIR. Bake for 20 minutes. If desired, sprinkle nuts on top and bake 10-15 more minutes or until brown. Bessie's liked to serve it with Blue Bell's Homemade Vanilla ice cream.

"Cooking is like painting or writing a song. Just as there are only so many notes or colors, there are only so many flavors --it's how you combine them that sets you apart."

Wolfgang Puck

4

Last Splash Mermaid Bachelorette Party

Midnight Kiss

Coconut Shrimp with Sweet Red Chili Sauce

"Sinsual" Mermen Balls

Pistachio Midori Bundt Cake

Mary and Maggie co-hosted a weekend bachelorette party for Mary's Phi Pi little sister, Carla. Most of their menu could be partially made a day ahead. Maggie decided to hire Todd, a local culinary student to help serve and do all the last-minute cooking. Todd also kept the ladies entertained, wearing only a G-string and a bib apron. He had previously worked as a male stripper in New Orleans, before enrolling in culinary school.

Midnight Kiss
Serves 2

6-ounces Tito's Vodka
2-ounces Blue Curacao
4-teaspoons of lemon juice
12-ounces of chilled
          Champagne
Sugar
Orange

Rim the edge of the Champagne flutes with an orange wedge. Roll in sugar to coat. Pour in vodka and cCampagne. Add blue curacao and garnish with an orange slice.

Coconut Shrimp with Sweet Red Chili Sauce
21-25 Shrimp

1/3 cups all-purpose flour
½ teaspoon salt and ½ teaspoon black pepper
1 tablespoon chopped cilantro (optional)
2 large eggs, beaten
¾ cup Panko bread crumbs
1 cup sweetened shredded coconut
1-pound large shrimp, peeled and deveined (21-25 shrimp per pound)
3-4 tablespoons vegetable or peanut oil
1/3 cup sweet Thai chili sauce
½ cup of orange marmalade
Finely chopped jalapeno (optional)

Peel and devein shrimp. It's optional if you want the tail to stay intact. In a small bowl mix flour, salt, pepper. In another small bowl beat the eggs. In a medium bowl combine Panko and coconut. In a Dutch oven, wok or skillet, add oil and heat over medium high heat. While oil is heating up, dip shrimp in flour, dunk in egg, dredge in Panko coconut mixture. Set dredged shrimp on platter until you have finished with the remaining shrimp. Fry the shrimp in small batches (4 to 6 at a time) until golden and crispy. Drain on a rack. Maggie placed the shrimp in a circle around the dipping sauce. She labeled the dish Cock "n" Nut Shrimp.

For dipping sauce combine Sweet Thai chili sauce, orange marmalade, and chopped jalapeno.

Recommended wines: *Pinot Grigio or Chardonnay*

Pamela Boleyn

Assorted Mermen Balls

Make sure to label each platter:

The Hulk aka Spinach Balls

The Terminator aka Bavarian Meatballs

The Southern Gent aka Sausage Pimento Cheese Balls

The Goat Man aka Goat Cheese Balls

The Hulk aka Spinach Balls
Yields 75 balls

2 (10 ounce) packages frozen chopped spinach
2 cups Pepperidge Farm Herb Stuffing
¾ cup unsalted butter, melted
5 beaten eggs
½ cup grated Parmesan cheese
1 Vidalia onion, minced
½ teaspoon garlic powder
1 teaspoon Italian seasoning
Salt and pepper to taste

Preheat oven to 350 degrees F. Microwave spinach according to package instructions. Allow spinach to cool slightly and then squeeze out as much liquid as possible, using a colander. Combine all ingredients and roll into 1 teaspoon balls. Bake balls on greased baking sheets for 20 minutes. Drain on rack or paper towels. Serve hot. May be frozen after cooking, just reheat 3-5 minutes at 400 degrees F.

Recommended wines: *Chardonnay or Spumante*

The Terminator aka Bavarian Balls
Yields 66 balls

1 32-ounce package of frozen Italian style cocktail size
meatballs
½ cup chopped onions
¼ cup brown sugar
1 envelope onion soup mix
1 can (12 ounces) Guinness Stout Beer

In a slow cooker, combine meatballs and onion.
Sprinkle brown sugar and soup mix on top. Pour beer over
top. Cover and cook on low for 5-6 hours. Stir well to coat the
meatballs. Serve with cocktail picks.

Recommended wines: *Chardonnay or Riesling
(medium-dry)*

The Southern Gent aka Sausage Pimento Cheese Balls
Yields 50 balls

1-pound of bulk ground pork sausage
2 ½ cups biscuit baking mix
1 ½ cups prepared pimiento cheese
2 tablespoons chopped fresh chives

Preheat oven 350 degrees F. Combine all ingredients in a medium bowl and mix well by hand. Shape mixture into 1-inch balls, and place on 2 baking sheets lined with parchment paper. Bake until lightly golden and firm, approximately 15 minutes. Serve warm or room temperature.

Recommended wines: *Chardonnay or Pinot Noir*

The Goat Man aka Goat Cheese Balls
24 balls

6 ounces goat cheese (softened)
4 ounces cream cheese (softened)
¾ cup coarsely chopped pecans
1 teaspoon extra-virgin olive oil
1 teaspoon of honey
½ teaspoon of Sriracha, a red chili hot sauce
¼ teaspoon of kosher salt
3 tablespoons dried cranberries
3 tablespoons golden raisins
1 tablespoon finely chopped fresh rosemary
3 tablespoons of finely chopped fresh parsley

Mix softened goat cheese and cream cheese in a food processor. Transfer to bowl; cover with plastic wrap and refrigerate at least one hour. Shape into 1 tablespoon balls. Preheat oven 325 degrees F. Line a baking pan with parchment paper. Combine pecans, oil, honey and Siracha on pan. Spread out mixture. Bake 3 minutes, stir pecan, then bake 3-5 more minutes, until pecans are lightly toasted. Stir in Kosher salt. Let mixture cool. In food processor, pulse cranberries, raisins, rosemary and parsley several times. Add pecan mixture and pulse several times until well mixed. Put mixture in a shallow pan. Roll balls in mixture. Store balls in air tight container in refrigerator. 30 minutes before serving remove from refrigerator to slightly soften them. Serve with crackers or crostini.

Recommended wines: *Riesling or Cava*

Pistachio Midori Bundt Cake

3/4 cup Midori liqueur
1 box yellow cake
1 (3 ounce) box instant pistachio pudding
4 eggs
½ cup plain yogurt or sour cream
½ cup vegetable oil
½ teaspoon coconut flavoring
½ cup chopped pistachios

Preheat oven 350 degrees F. Mix and beat all ingredients for 4 minutes at medium speed. Pour into a well-greased Bundt cake pan. Bake for 50-55 minutes. Cool 15 minutes in pan, then turn out onto cooling rack. Glaze while still warm. Sprinkle top with pistachios.

Glaze:
2 cups powdered sugar
½ cup Midori liqueur
4 ounces cream cheese, softened
2 tablespoons of unsalted butter, softened
½ teaspoon of coconut flavoring

Mix and beat at high speed until smooth and spreadable.

*"Cooking is at once child's play and adult joy.
And cooking done with care is an act of love."*

Craig Claiborne

5

Sharon's Cinco de Mayo Party

Spicy Jalapeno Margaritas

Sharon's Easy 7-Layer Dip

Pineapple Strawberry Salsa

Zucchini and Eggplant Enchiladas with Spicy Black Bean Sauce

Cilantro Lime Rice

Chocolate Avocado Mousse

For large parties, Sharon sets up a self-serve Margarita bar. She pre-makes several batches of Margaritas and serves them in a small punch bowl. Next to the punch bowl there is an ice bucket and pink Himalayan salt, so the guests can rim their glasses. Also, extra orange juice, Champagne, sparkling water, and sliced limes so that her guests can add more to their drink or make mimosas instead.

Sharon's menu is somewhat time consuming, because of the chopping involved. The day before she invites a friend over, and they make the mousse and prep many of the ingredients. The enchiladas are assembled, covered, refrigerated overnight. One hour before baking the casserole, she removes it from refrigerator and lets it rest. After she uncovers the casserole it's ready to be baked in a preheated oven.

Spicy Jalapeno Margaritas
Serves 4

¾ cup silver tequila
¼ to ½ jalapeno pepper
½ cup of Grand Marnier
½ cup fresh lime juice
¼ cup fresh squeezed orange juice

Pour the tequila into a small glass pitcher. Add the sliced jalapeno, amount determined on how spicy you want the drink to be. Let set for 15 minutes or longer if you want more heat. Mix tequila with remaining ingredients and serve on the rocks.

Sharon's Easy Vegan 7-Layer Dip
16 servings

2 (14-ounce) cans vegetarian refried black beans
2 teaspoons cumin
1/3 cup water (or more so beans will be creamy)
2 cups guacamole (store bought is fine)
2 large limes
1 teaspoon sea salt
2 cups Tofutti Sour Cream
2 cups Pico de Gallo salsa
1 (11- ounce) can shoe peg corn, drained
1 cup Roma tomatoes, seeded and diced
1 (2.25-ounce) can, sliced black olives, drained
4 green onions sliced
Fresh chopped cilantro

    In mixing bowl or food processor, mash refried beans. Add cumin and water, mixing well. Put beans in the bottom of large but shallow clear glass dish. Layer in this order, guacamole, sour cream, salsa, corn, tomatoes, green onions, and olives. Top with cilantro. Serve with tortilla chips.

Pineapple Strawberry Salsa
6 servings

Whole pineapple (to use as fruit salsa bowl)
1 cup of diced pineapple
1 cup of fresh strawberries diced
1 cup red pepper, cored, seeded and finely diced
¼ cup red onion finely diced
1 medium jalapeno, cored, seeded and finely diced
1/3 cup fresh cilantro, chopped
4 tablespoons fresh lime juice
¼ teaspoon sea salt
¼ teaspoon black pepper

To make pineapple bowl, cut long ways cut 1/3 of the pineapple off leaving stem intact. Lay the larger section on its side and remove fruit leaving a 1/2 -in shell. Pour juice out of pineapple bowl but reserving it. Remove fruit from the smaller section.

Dice 1 cup of pineapple for salsa. Save rest for other use. In medium bowl mix pineapple, strawberries, red pepper, red onion, jalapeno, lime juice, salt, and pepper. Transfer to pineapple bowl. Serve with tortilla chips.

Zucchini and Eggplant Enchiladas
Makes 16 Enchiladas

Cooking spray
4 medium zucchinis, diced
2 medium eggplants, with skin on diced
1 teaspoon sea salt, divided
1/2 teaspoon black pepper
2 tablespoons olive oil
1 sweet onion, chopped
1 medium green bell pepper, seeded and diced
1 medium red pepper, seeded and diced
1 teaspoon paprika
1 teaspoon cumin
½ teaspoon chili powder
2 (15-ounce) cans reduced sodium black beans, partly drained
2 (15-ounce) cans reduced sodium fire roasted tomatoes
½ teaspoon cayenne pepper
½ teaspoon dried chipotle
16 (8-inch) flour or corn tortillas
2 packages of grated vegan jack cheese
Chopped green onions and fresh cilantro for garnish

Preheat oven 400 degrees F. Spray two baking sheets with cooking spray. Arrange a single layer eggplant and zucchini on baking sheets. Spray more cooking spray and sprinkle eggplant and zucchini with ½ teaspoon salt and ½ teaspoon pepper. Roast in oven about 25 minutes until cooked. Flip over after 10 minutes. Remove from oven and set aside in large bowl. Reduce oven to 350 degrees F. Heat olive oil in large skillet, add onion, peppers, paprika, cumin, chili powder. Cook until tender about 5 minutes. Add to bowl. In food processor blend black beans, roasted tomatoes, ½ tsp

salt, cayenne, and chipotle. Cover the bottom of two casserole baking dished with just enough sauce to cover. Fill each tortilla with the mixture, roll up, and lay enchiladas seam side down in pans. Spoon the remaining sauce on top. Bake for about 25 minutes and sprinkle with cheese. Continue baking until cheese melts and casserole is slightly bubbly. Garnish with chopped green onions and cilantro.

Cilantro Lime Rice
6 servings

2 tablespoons extra virgin olive oil
1 ½ cups basmati rice
1 clove garlic, minced
2 ¼ cups of water
1 teaspoon sea salt
Zest of 1 lime
3 tablespoons lime juice
1 cup (lightly packed) chopped cilantro leaves
3 thinly sliced green onions
Pinch of red pepper flakes (optional)

Heat the olive oil in a medium saucepan on medium heat. Add rice and stir to coat with oil. Stir frequently, until rice starts to brown. Add garlic and cook 1 minute. Add water, salt, lime zest, and bring to a boil. Cover and cook on low heat 15 minutes. Remove from heat and let rest for 10 minutes. Fluff with fork. Transfer to serving bowl. Pour lime juice over rice and toss in cilantro, green onions and red pepper flakes.

Chocolate Avocado Mousse
4 Servings

4 pitted dates
2 large ripe avocados sliced in half with seeds discarded
¼ cup unsweetened cocoa powder
1 teaspoon real vanilla
½ cup unsweetened almond drinking milk
½ teaspoon cinnamon
¼ teaspoon cayenne pepper
¼ teaspoon chili powder
¼ teaspoon sea salt

Place dates in small bowl and cover with water for 30-60 minutes. Discard water. In food processor blend together dates, avocado, cocoa powder, almond milk, vanilla. Add spices and salt. Pulse until creamy. Pour into small cups or ramekins. Refrigerate for 30 minutes or up to 2 days before serving. When ready to serve, dollop with coconut whipped cream and garnish with chocolate shavings.

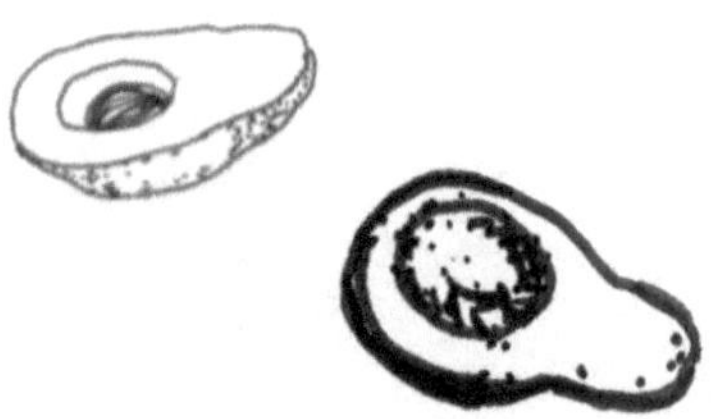

Coconut Whipped Cream

Important! Refrigerate overnight a 14-ounce canned full fat coconut milk until solidified.

1 (14-ounce) can full fat coconut milk
1/3 cup organic powdered sugar
Dark chocolate shavings for garnish

Drain water from the canned coconut milk and place the solid cream in a large chilled mixing bowl. Beat for 30 seconds with hand mixer. Add sugar and mix until smooth, about 1 minute. Taste and adjust sweetness if needed. Avoid over mixing because it will cause separations. Store in refrigerator until ready to serve.

*"The more you know, the more you can create.
There's no end to imagination in the kitchen."*

Julia Childs

6

SIXTY PINK RIBBONS RECEPTION

Pink Prosecco

Cosmopolitans

Norwegian Smoked Salmon Canapes

Boiled Shrimp with Pink Remoulade Sauce

Prosciutto and Melon Crostini

Strawberry Fudge Truffles

Maggie planned a unique event to celebrate Sharon's battle with breast cancer. The caterer used a pink (a symbol for surviving cancer) menu theme for the evening: pink Prosecco, pink cocktails, smoked salmon canapes, boiled shrimp with pink remoulade sauce, prosciutto and melon, and strawberry fudge truffles. The servers dressed in all black and wore pink carnation boutonnieres. A harpist played baroque music.

Classic Cosmopolitan
1 Serving

2-ounce vodka
½-ounce triple sec
¾-ounce cranberry juice cocktail
¼- ounce fresh lime juice (may want to increase to ½-oz)
1 orange peel twist
Ice

Fill a cocktail shaker with ice. Add vodka, triple sec, cranberry juice and lime juice. Shake for about 30 seconds. Strain into a martini glass. Garnish with orange peel twist.

Norwegian Smoked Salmon Canapes

12-ounce Norwegian Smoked Salmon
8-ounce cream cheese spread
2 tablespoons Crème fraîche
2 lemons zested
1 bunch of dill
Rye bread cut into small circles and lightly toasted
Black pepper

Mix the cream cheese, crème fraîche, lemon juice, and half of the lemon zest. Place on top of rye bread, using a fork to make a swirl pattern. Cut salmon into ½-in wide ribbons, then roll and twist into roses. Place on top of cream cheese spread. Top each with individual sprigs of dill and a couple of strands of lemon zest.

Recommended wines: *Prosecco or Chenin Blanc*

Prosciutto and Melon Crostini
6 Servings

French bread baguette
2-3 tablespoons extra-virgin olive oil
3 ounces Prosciutto di Parma, thin-sliced, cured ham
1 cantaloupe
1 cup whole milk ricotta cheese
1 cup Modena Balsamic vinegar
2/3 cup sugar
Basil

To make crostini, preheat oven to 450 degrees F. Line a large, rimmed baking sheet with parchment paper. Slice baguette on the diagonal into pieces no wider than ½-inch. Lightly brush both sides with oil and place in a single layer on baking sheet. Bake on middle rack for 6 to 9 minutes, until crisp and golden. To make a balsamic glaze, combine vinegar and sugar in a small saucepan. Bring to boil, then reduce to simmer, stirring often until vinegar has thickened and coats back of spoon. Cool down to room temperature. Peel melon and scoop out the seeds. Cut into wedges and use a vegetable peeler to slice thinly so melon can be folded. Slice prosciutto half lengthwise. Whip ricotta until smooth. To assemble layer on each baguette a spoonful of ricotta, a folded slice of prosciutto and top with a folded slice of cantaloupe. Lightly drizzle with balsamic glaze and a sprinkle of chiffonade basil.

To chiffonade basil, stack several basil leaves on top of each other and roll tightly. While holding the roll, slice crosswise, cutting the roll into very thin strips.

Recommended wines: Rose' or Chardonnay

Strawberry Fudge Truffles
48 Pieces

6-ounce semi-sweet chocolate chips
½ cup almonds, toasted and finely chopped
8-ounce cream cheese, at room temperature
¾ cup vanilla wafer crumbs
¼ cup strawberry preserves

In a small pan, over low heat melt chocolate. In medium bowl beat cream cheese until creamy. Add melted chocolate, beating until smooth. Stir in vanilla wafer crumbs and preserves, mixing well. Cover and chill for 1 hour. Remove from refrigerator and shape into 1-inch balls. Roll balls into the almond chips. Chill until serving time.

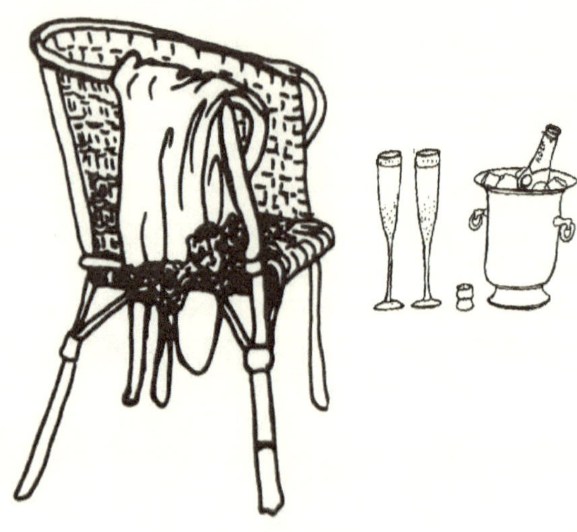

"Cooking is like love.

It should be entered into with abandon or not at all."

Harriet Van Horne

7

John's Romantic Dinner For Two

Chappellet Merlot Napa Valley 2002

Grilled Summer Vegetables Over Orzo Pilaf

Grilled Lamb Chops

Dark Chocolate Fondue with Bananas, Figs, & Strawberries

As she came down from the stairs, Alabama's Mountain Music was playing. Maggie had every album Alabama had released. She yelled down, "Something smells incredibly wonderful."

John replied, "I'm pan grilling some New Zealand lamp chops. Sit down... I'll pour you a glass of Merlot."

Grilled Summer Vegetables Over Orzo
Serves 4

3 cups low-sodium chicken broth
1 cup orzo
1 teaspoon chopped fresh rosemary
Extra-virgin oil
1 Vidalia onion, cut into ½-in slices
2 yellow squash, halved lengthwise
2 zucchini squash, halved lengthwise
2 Roma tomatoes, halved and seeded
2 tablespoons olive oil
2 teaspoons cider vinegar
½ teaspoon chopped fresh parsley
½ teaspoon chopped fresh thyme
¼ teaspoon kosher salt
¼ cup crumbled goat cheese

In a saucepan add a tablespoon of olive oil and toast orzo until lightly brown. Add broth and rosemary pan and bring to a simmer over medium-low heat. Cook 25 minutes or until liquid is absorbed. Remove from heat. Brush vegetables with olive oil. Grill vegetables until tender, approximately 5 minutes. Grill tomatoes skin side down and do not turn over. Turn the onions and squash over midway. (John used a cast iron grill pan.) Remove vegetables to cookie sheet and keep warm in oven while lamb is grilled. (Lamb recipe follows.)

When lamb is done, cut vegetables in bite size pieces. In large bowl whisk together 2 tablespoons olive oil, parsley thyme, and salt. Add vegetables, tossing gently to coat. Spread the cooked orzo on a serving platter. Top with grilled vegetables and sprinkle with goat cheese. Any leftovers are great served cold.

Grilled Lamb Rib Chops
Serves 2

2 tablespoons extra-virgin olive oil
2 large garlic cloves
1 tablespoon coarsely chopped fresh rosemary leaves
½ teaspoon sea salt
Pinch of cracked black pepper
Pinch of white pepper
6 lamb rib chops

In a food processor, blend together olive oil, garlic, rosemary, sea salt, white pepper and black pepper to form a marinade paste. Rub paste on chops and marinate at least 1 hour. Heat grill pan over high heat and add chops. Sear 2 minutes on each side. Reduce heat to medium and cook chops until desired doneness, about 3 minutes per side for medium-rare. Transfer to a platter, tent with foil, and rest chops for 5 minutes before cutting.

Recommended wines: *Merlot or Syrah*

Dark Chocolate Fondue
Serves 8

10-ounce bag of Ghirardelli's bittersweet chocolate chips
2/3 cup heavy cream
1 teaspoon Madagascar vanilla extract
¼ teaspoon sea salt

In a medium saucepan at low heat, combine chocolate chips and cream. Stir constantly until chocolate melts and mixture is smooth. Stir in vanilla and salt. If you wish sauce to be thinner add additional cream until desired consistency. Pour into fondue pot to keep sauce warm.

Great served with bananas, figs and strawberries.

Recommended wines: *Merlot or Pinot Noir (oaked)*

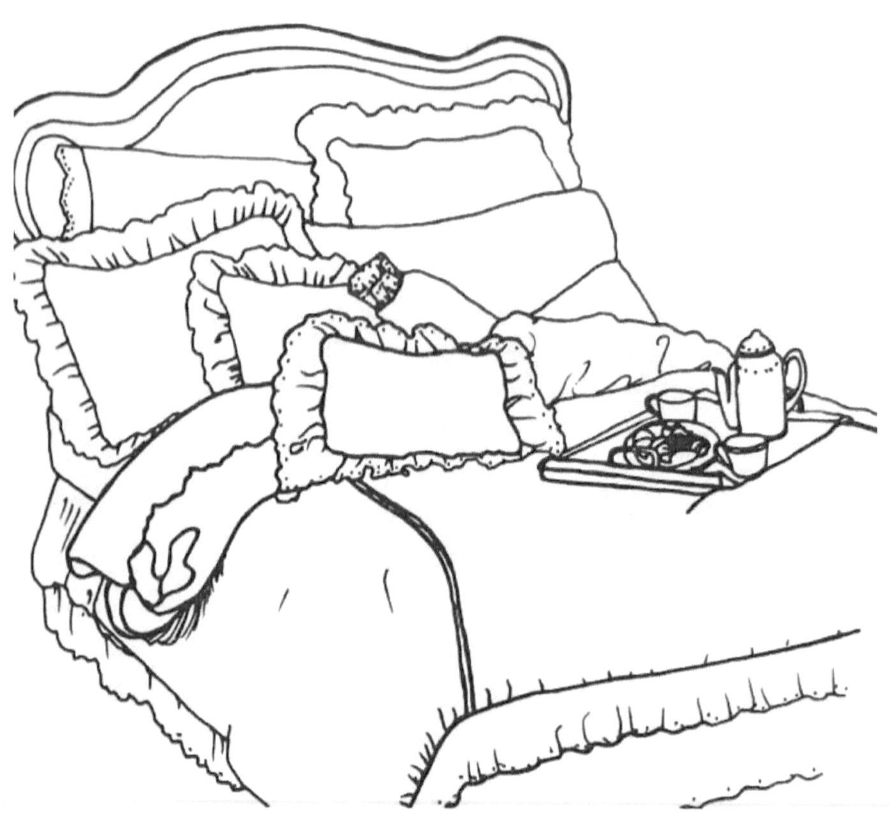

*"My weaknesses have always been food
and men-in that order."*

Dolly Parton

8

The Morning After

Whiskey Willy's Bloody Mary

Sean's Eggs Benedict with Hollandaise Sauce

Seasonal Fruit

*A few staples to stock
in case of an unexpected sleep over:*

Coffee, Cream and Sugar

Eggs

Bread, preferable English Muffins or Bagels

Pancake Mix, Syrup, and Jam or Jelly

Bacon, Sausage or Canadian bacon

Yogurt

Avocados for Avocado Toast

Granola

Bananas

Champagne, Orange Juice, Bloody Mary Mix, Vodka

Sean's Eggs Benedict with Hollandaise Sauce
Serves 2

2 English muffins, halved and toasted
4 slices Canadian bacon
4 large eggs
Hollandaise sauce
Cayenne pepper
Chopped chives to garnish
Paprika to garnish

Hollandaise Sauce:
3 tablespoons butter
3 eggs yolks
1 teaspoons lemon juice
Tabasco, a splash-to taste (optional)
Salt and pepper to taste

First make the Hollandaise Sauce. Melt butter in small saucepan. In separate bowl, beat egg yolks. Mix in lemon juice, salt and pepper. Gradually whisk in, a small spoonful at a time, the hot butter to temper the eggs. When finished, pour mixture back into sauce pan. Cook on low heat, stirring constantly, for 20-30 seconds. Remove from heat and set aside so it will thicken. For a little kick, add Tabasco.

Poach the Eggs:
4 large eggs
1 teaspoon white vinegar

Fill medium size pot with about 3 inches of water. Bring water to a boil and then reduce heat until water simmers. Add vinegar. Crack each egg and gently lower eggs into simmering water. Cook approximately 3-5 minutes until the whites are firm but yolks are runny. Remove the eggs with a slotted spoon and hold over a kitchen towel until drained.

While the eggs are cooking, heat 4 slices of Canadian bacon in fry pan on medium-high heat, about 1 minute per side.

Top each muffin with a slice of bacon, then a poached egg. Top with hollandaise sauce and garnish with chopped chives. Sprinkle with paprika.

"Food is romantic. Soul. It's about putting everything in your heart onto the plate. Hoping it's perceived well. Honestly, it's about passion. It's about love."

Hillary Sterling

9

Sean's Candlelight Dinner

Santa Margherita Pinot Grigio

Garlic Bread

Mixed Green Salad with Sweet Italian Dressing

Sean's Linguini with Clam Sauce

Tiramisu for Two

Sambuca Shots

This dinner is quite simple to make. There are also several shortcuts to make it even easier. You can substitute frozen garlic bread and buy a bag of mixed greens for the salad. Many grocery stores like Publix and Fresh Market offer Tiramisu in their bakery. Costco's Dessert Italiano Tiramisu even comes in a reusable glass cup.

Garlic Bread
Serves Two

2 slices of Italian Bread- cut one inch thick
1 tablespoon of butter at room temperature
2 cloves of garlic, minced
Pinch of onion salt
¼ teaspoon dried basil
1 tablespoon Parmigiano Reggiano cheese

Mix butter, garlic, onion salt, and basil. Spread on one side of bread and sprinkle with cheese. Spread to combine. Place bread on baking sheet, garlic side up and broil until toasted.

Sweet Italian Salad Dressing

½ cup red wine vinegar
2 tablespoons honey
1 teaspoon dried Italian seasoning
2 cloves of garlic minced
Pinch of sea salt
Pinch of cracked black pepper
½ extra virgin olive oil

Place vinegar, honey, Italian seasoning, garlic, salt and pepper in a blender. While blender is running, slowly drizzle oil until dressing emulsified. Adjust seasoning if necessary, or add more oil if you want it less acid. Serve over a mixed green salad.

Sean's Linguini with Clam Sauce
Serves Four

3 green onions, chopped
4 cloves of garlic, minced
2 tablespoons of fresh parsley, chopped
½ cup unsalted butter
Splash of dry white wine
4 (6 ½ ounce) cans minced clams
½ cup heavy whipping cream
¼ teaspoon Kosher salt
Linguini
Parmigiano Reggiano cheese
Cracked black pepper to taste

Cook linguini al dente, reserving 2 ounces of pasta water for sauce. Sauté onions and garlic in butter for 1-2 minutes until translucent. Add a splash of dry white wine. Add clams in their juice, whipping cream, salt, and ¼ cup of Parmigiano Reggiano cheese. Add reserve pasta water and linguine. Cook over medium heat until thoroughly heated. Top with grated Parmigiano Reggiano and cracked pepper to taste.

Recommended wines: *Chardonnay or Pinot Gris*

Tiramisu
For Two

4 ounces full fat mascarpone cheese
2 tablespoons granulated sugar
½ teaspoon vanilla extract
½ cup heavy whipping cream
½ cup chilled strong coffee
1 tablespoon granulated sugar
Cocoa powder
Ladyfingers

In bowl, whisk mascarpone cheese and 2 tablespoons of sugar. Add vanilla and whipping cream and continue mixing until it becomes a stiff cream. Soak ladyfingers in coffee for a few seconds. Arrange in bottom of two 1-cup glass bowls. Dust with cocoa powder. Spoon half mascarpone mixture in two glass bowls. Add another layer of soaked ladyfingers and rest of mascarpone. Chill in the refrigerator 1-2 hours. Dust top with cocoa powder before serving.

Recommended after-dinner drink: Sambuca served with three coffee beans floating on top to signify health, happiness, and prosperity.

Sambuca Shots

Sambuca is an Italian anise-flavored liqueur. When serving the shot of Sambuca remember to add three coffee beans, each representing health, happiness and prosperity.

"It's okay to play with your food."

Emeril Lagasse

10

Maggie O' Book Club

Fun Book Club Tips

Plan the menu around a theme that relates to the book. Suggest to everyone they come dressed as one of the book's characters. In Maggie O', Seven Years Forgotten, there could be several different themes. The variety of wonderful settings should influence your menu.

Also, there are almost 50 food dishes as well as many types of wine and specialty cocktails mentioned in the book. Several suggested beverages for a Maggie O' theme event include Prosecco, Santa Margherita Pinot Grigio, Siduri Pinot Noir, or for a brunch event, Whiskey Willy's Bloody Mary.

Following are several appetizer recipes that I've found easy to make. You might also want to bake some ever-popular Toll House Chocolate Chip Cookies.

Mini Black Olive Pizzas
18-20 mini pizzas

1 ball refrigerated store bought pizza dough
1 jar of marinara sauce
Pitted black olives, sliced
Shredded part-skim mozzarella cheese
Crushed red pepper flakes, for serving

Preheat oven 400 degrees F. Line a large baking sheet with parchment paper. Place pizza dough on a well-floured surface, press dough firmly with your fingers to shape, and stretch gently into a 12" x 8" rectangle. With a round biscuit cutter, cut dough into 18-20 rounds; place rounds 1 inch apart on baking sheet. Top each with sauce, cheese, and olives. Bake for 8-10 minutes, or until cheese is melted.

Pizza is mentioned 21 times in the novel.

Bloody Mary Pickled Shrimp
Serves 8

Whiskey Willy's Bloody Mary Mix and three different shrimp dishes are referenced in the novel.

This is a great dish to make for any special occasion. It can be made in advance and stored covered in the refrigerator for up to two days.

1 (32 ounce) bottle Whiskey Willy's Bloody Mary Mix
2 ½ pounds medium peeled, deveined raw shrimp
4 cups of ice
½ cup cocktail sauce
1/3 cup vodka
1/3 cup olive oil
1/3 cup fresh lemon juice
1 tablespoon Tabasco
1 tablespoon Worcestershire
1 teaspoon celery seeds
1 teaspoon black pepper
1 cup thinly sliced celery
1 cup thinly sliced Vidalia onion
Garnish: celery leaves and lemon slices

Place 1 cup of water and 3 cups of Bloody Mary mix in large sauce pan. Bring to boil. Remove from heat. Add shrimp cover and let stand until shrimp are barely opaque in center. Stir ice into shrimp. Let stand until shrimp are cool. Drain shrimp and pat dry. Stir together cocktail sauce, vodka, oil, lemon juice, Tabasco, Worcestershire, celery seeds, pepper, and the remaining Bloody Mary mix in a large heavy-duty freezer bag. Add shrimp, celery and onions. Seal bag and refrigerate at least 8 hours, preferably, up to 24 hours. Transfer to large serving bowl and top with celery leaves and lemon slices.

Pamela Boleyn

Hot Reuben Dip
Serves 8

8-ounce package of cream cheese softened
8-ounce deli corned beef coarsely chopped
1 cup of Swiss cheese shredded
½ cup sauerkraut drained well
¼ cup sour cream
¼ cup Thousand Island dressing

What can be more New York than Reuben sandwiches. This recipe is so easy to make! Combine all the ingredients in a crockpot. Cook on high for 2 to 3 hours or low for 4 to 6 hours. Serve with Triscuit crackers or Melba rye chips.

Maggie's Pimento Cheese
Tea Sandwiches

2 cups Extra Sharp Cheddar Cheese hand shredded
1 cup Monterey Jack Cheese hand shredded
4-ounces cream cheese, softened to room temperature
½ cup mayonnaise
1/8 cup chopped onions (Vidalia if available)
¼ teaspoon of cayenne pepper. Add more if you want
        more heat.
¼ teaspoon of garlic powder
¼ teaspoon of salt
¼ teaspoon of pepper
¼ teaspoon of paprika
4-ounce jar of diced pimentos, drained
White sandwich bread-do not use end slices.

It's easier to make pimento cheese in a food processor but you can also use a mixer or by hand. In the bowl of a food processor fitted with the steel blade, combine the cream cheese, mayonnaise, onions, and all the spices. Process until smooth and evenly combined. Add 1 cup of the Cheddar cheese and ½ cup of the Monterey Jack cheese. Process until smooth, scraping sides as needed. Add the remaining cheese and the pimento. Pulse several times, then stir to blend mixture. Taste and adjust seasoning, if necessary. Spread filling on one piece of bread and top with a second piece of bread, pressing down gently. Cut the crusts off the bread and cut each sandwich into triangles. Cover with a damp tea towel until guest arrive.

A secret to making pimento cheese is to NEVER use pre-shredded cheese. Always shred it, using a box grater. Not only is block cheese cheaper, but it also doesn't contain additives and tastes much better than pre-shredded cheese.

Pamela Boleyn

If you want to make sandwiches ahead of time, cover them tightly with plastic wrap and keep them in the refrigerator. Chilling the sandwiches makes them easier to cut.

You may recall that as Maggie was eating a pimento cheese sandwich for lunch, when she saw Christopher being interviewed by Dixie Reynolds.

Fruit Kabobs with Margarita Dip
Serves Twelve

6-ounces cream cheese, softened
8-ounces sour cream
½ cup confectioner's sugar
2 tablespoons lime juice
2 tablespoons of thawed frozen orange juice concentrate
2 tablespoons of silver tequila
1 cup heavy whipping cream
24 fresh strawberries
12 pineapple chunks
2 medium mangos, peeled and cubed
12 seedless red grapes
4 slices poundcake cubed

Margarita Dip:
>   In a large bowl combine first six ingredients.
>   Beat in whipping cream until fluffy.
>   Thread fruit and pound cake on 12 wooden skewers.

Serving a recipe like this is great since it can be made ahead, is easy to serve, and is very colorful. Feel free to substitute other fruit. The Margarita Dip is also great with salted Pretzel Crisps.

The Author

Pamela Boleyn released her first novel, *Maggie O' Seven Years Forgotten* in December 2019. Soon afterwards, she found out she had early-stage breast cancer. Fortunately, it was detected in her annual mammogram.

A hopeless romantic, the author intertwines her Southern roots with her passion for cooking, art and travel into her vivid stories. Ms. Boleyn is currently working on *Maggie O'-The Backstory,*.a prequel to her first novel.

In *Dining & Entertaining Maggie O' Style*, Ms. Boleyn created ten themed menus based on the idiosyncratic personalities of Maggie O' and her supporting cast, Bessie, John, Mary, Sharon, Ron, Matthew, and Sean. While this unique style entertainment guide is a great standalone recipe collection, it is meant to be an enjoyable reading companion to Ms. Boleyn's first novel.

When not writing, Ms. Boleyn operates a catering business with her significant other, who is also an experienced professional chef. Their catering business specializes in Coastal Southern and Mediterranean cuisine.

Bon Appetit!

Recipe Index

Cocktail Time

Small Sexy Bites

Big Boy Bites

Buttermilk Fried Oysters, 17
Chicken & Conecuh Sausage Gumbo, 30
Grilled Lamb Rib Chops, 65
New York, New York Bagel Station, 23
Sean's Eggs Benedict with Hollandaise Sauce, 70
Sean's Linguini with Clam Sauce, 76
Shrimp and Grits Casserole, 18
Zucchini & Eggplant Enchiladas, 51

Side Dishes

Cilantro Lime Rice, 53
Cheese Grits Casserole, 25
Creole Mustard Potato Salad, 31
Garlic Bread, 74
Grilled Summer Vegetables Over Orzo Pilaf, 64
Honey Butter, 34
Pineapple Strawberry Salsa, 50
Southern Buttermilk Cornbread, 33
Southern Collard Greens, 32
Sweet Italian Salad Dressing, 75

93

Sweet Temptations

Chilton County Peach Cobbler, 35
Chocolate Avocado Mousse, 54
Coconut Whipped Cream, 55
Dark Chocolate Fondue, 66
Pistachio Midori Bundt Cake, 45
Strawberry Fudge Truffles, 61
Strawberry Margarita Key Lime Pie, 19
Tiramisu For Two, 77